London Fling's

Mihir Otia

BLUEROSE PUBLISHERS
India | U.K.

Copyright © Mihir Otia 2024

All rights reserved by author. No part of this publication may be reproduced, stored in a retrieval system or transmitted in any form or by any means, electronic, mechanical, photocopying, recording or otherwise, without the prior permission of the author. Although every precaution has been taken to verify the accuracy of the information contained herein, the publisher assumes no responsibility for any errors or omissions. No liability is assumed for damages that may result from the use of information contained within.

BlueRose Publishers takes no responsibility for any damages, losses, or liabilities that may arise from the use or misuse of the information, products, or services provided in this publication.

For permissions requests or inquiries regarding this publication, please contact:

BLUEROSE PUBLISHERS
www.BlueRoseONE.com
info@bluerosepublishers.com
+91 8882 898 898
+4407342408967

ISBN: 978-93-6783-819-8

Cover Design: Sadhna Kumari
Typesetting: Pooja Sharma

First Edition: October 2024

DEDICATION

वक्रतुण्ड महाकाय सूर्यकोटि समप्रभ
निर्विघ्नं कुरु मे देव सर्वकार्येषु सर्वदा

London Flings, Ahh!!! The book closet to my heart my dream works to which the worth it is to read the more it was for me to write and recreate all the dialogue's which somehow have crossed my paths ever since.

I Would love to dedicate this book to the Otia Family My Grandfather Jitendra AKA Jitudada My Parents Mrs. Jayshree and Mr Kedar, My elder brother Mr Dhaval and my dearly Nephew Riddish.

My friends and my partners Mr Deep Panchal and Mr Harshal Patel.

Above All my Love, my better half Miss Charmi Shah Otia – A true love and my soul mate which is the highlight of the whole journey whether it's London Flings or Just a guy at the bar she's always there for me and the success of this book, Thank you So much Love it really takes me to our childhood to where it all started and hope for the best in the future P.S..I LOVE YOU!!!

Zealous for **Midehar Med Care LLP.**

SUMMARY

A fictional book on the plot where Leo a teen adult from India is so broken from his breakup that he is so miserable and over attached to the girl he loved but after getting a heart break his impression of love has changed and now what he is looking for is his outrage on career and sports begin a best neuroscientist is his one goal and to play tennis is now his routine to smash all his anger on the court he tries to accomplish everything he sees and want to succeed in his life like no other girl can ever reject him, at this time he already lost his friends so now a the lone wolf is out there hunting for any blood that draws his attention in this the very first girl comes to his life as a fling is mona with whom he experiences a lot of sex whether it is a lonely road or a rainy night or a mountain morning or else it be a hotel room by this he comes across a beauty at his work bhargi with whom his first eye contact was a magic and he imagined a lot of lust with her by dropping he home having car sex or sharing a cigarette after sex whether in middle of a Sunday afternoon he would call bhargi to have sex at her place and night he would go to mona to have a sound sleep, interestingly he got transferred to Bangalore and there on his way he found his third fling Rita with whom the Bangalore he saw was more red than green to settle his lust on his tennis matcha days he found out another fling Racheal who was divorced with a kid and the sex he experienced with her was the best for his sports to boost out. having so many flings in the middle of everything he decided to move to London and he got his ways to settle each fling in his sexy manners to make sure he has a remembrance when he moves to London, during his flight to London he met a girl from Delhi and started to have chat with her and he made sure that she would fall for him in any circumstances but he was destined to have someone waiting for him at the airport Sabar who was his guidance for his London dream but on the fling but his life changes on the flight as turbulence occur he runs to emergency outlet where he finds the charm he was missing the love of his life Sharmi with whom he recalled all his childhood days she hugged him so tight that he anger his flings his lust all just vanished and his heart starting beating again but the road to sharmi was difficult than it seems for a year in London he never had a chance to meet sharmi and till then he started to be the wolf again that was fuelled by Sabar but one day the stars aligned to his favour and it was the day he met sharmi after one whole year with tears and love in his heart sharmi pulled the love in him and that day was the day when Leo finally found peace and started to settle they moved in together started to have a relationship but the families were against this love so Leo decided to move to New York with sharmi to settle away from everyone and start their new love story they then have a daughter and he named her Harshita to which the daughter was the beautiful result of this two who have had a tough relationship but which they made a life and they lived happily ever after.

CONTENTS

RISING OF THE SUN 1

THERE IS A DIFFERENT SUN IN INDIA............................ 11

THE SUN RISES BEYOND THE CLOUD 22

THE BANGALORE CONNECTION 35

LET'S GO TO LONDON 44

LONDON FOG THE LONG-DISTANCE LOVE 58

WINTER NIGHTS IN LONDON THE CROSSROADS
OF COMMITMENT 69

THE SHINING SUN -THE PROPOSAL 74

HOWAY NEW YORK- TRIALS AND TRIUMPHS................ 80

THE EVOLUTION OF LOVE 91

LIFE AS PREDICTED A PERFECT ENDING........................ 98

1

RISING OF THE SUN

Leo, a young man from India, stood at the intersection of his past and future. His heart, once overflowing with love, was now shattered, leaving behind fragments that dug deep into his soul. It had been a painful breakup, one that reshaped his entire being. For months, he had adored the girl, built dreams around her, and imagined a future where nothing could go wrong. But in a blink, it all crumbled.

Love had betrayed him.

Heartbreak twisted his perception of love, transforming it from a pure emotion into something dark, something that needed to be kept at arm's length. And as the pain of rejection devoured him, Leo's mind began to seek something else—something to fill the void. He found his release on the tennis court. His rage and sadness poured out with every strike of the racket, each smash carrying the weight of his anger and the remnants of his affection.

But tennis was not enough. The burn inside him needed more fuel, and his career ambitions quickly turned into an obsession. The once timid, romantic boy was gone, replaced by someone cold, calculating—a man who vowed to never be rejected again. His new goal: become the best neuroscientist the world had ever seen. He would succeed so fiercely that no one—no woman—could ever turn him down again.

Leo stood by the window, the cold glass pressed against his forehead, as the evening sun dipped below the horizon. Outside, the streets of Mumbai buzzed with life, yet inside his small apartment, everything felt eerily silent. It had been a month since Priya had walked out of his life, leaving behind a gaping hole that echoed with the memories of their time together. The photos on the wall, once vibrant reminders of happy moments, now felt like ghosts haunting his every thought.

Their relationship had been a whirlwind of passion and promise, a love that Leo had believed would last forever. They had shared dreams and plans for the future—traveling the world, building a life together, and even having a family. But as the months wore on, reality set in. Priya had ambitions of her own, dreams that extended far beyond the small-town life they had envisioned together. She wanted to explore, to see the world without the constraints of a relationship, and eventually, that desire led her to make the heart-wrenching decision to end things.

The breakup had shattered him. Every time he closed his eyes, he could still hear the tremor in her voice as she spoke those dreaded words. "I need to find myself, Leo. I can't do that while I'm with you." He replayed that moment in his mind, wishing he could have changed her mind, wishing he could have promised her the world. But promises felt empty now, like whispers carried away by the wind.

In the weeks that followed, Leo withdrew into himself. Friends who had once filled his life with laughter and joy slowly faded into the background. He couldn't bear to see them, couldn't face the questions that always came. "Are you okay?" "Have you talked to her?" Each inquiry felt like a dagger, reopening the wound that had yet to heal. So he became a recluse, shutting out the world and burying himself in work. His job at the neuroscience research lab was demanding, but it was also a refuge. The sterile environment, filled with the whirring of machines and the quiet hum of intellect, offered him solace. Here, he could focus on something that made sense, something that didn't require emotional investment.

As he navigated the lonely days, the ache of heartbreak morphed into anger. It fueled him in ways he hadn't anticipated. Instead of wallowing in sorrow, he channeled his energy into his work. He began to push himself harder, often staying late at the lab, losing himself in research papers and experiments. He wanted to prove to himself that he could succeed without Priya. He wanted to build a life that no one could ever take away from him again.

But the anger wasn't solely directed at Priya. It was a rage that seeped into every aspect of his life. He became increasingly frustrated with the people around him, snapping at colleagues for trivial matters, isolating himself further. It was as if the heartbreak had stripped away his ability to connect with anyone. Instead, he became a ghost of his former self—a lone wolf hunting for a sense of purpose in a world that felt increasingly foreign.

At night, when the weight of his solitude became too heavy to bear, he turned to physical outlets. Leo had always enjoyed playing tennis, a sport he had picked up in high school. Now, he found solace on the court, smashing balls with a ferocity that matched the turmoil in his heart. The sound of the racket hitting the ball was cathartic, a way to vent the anger that threatened to consume him. He started training more frequently, becoming almost obsessive about improving his game. Tennis became his therapy, the only place where he felt he could exert control over something, anything, in his life.

But even the court couldn't fully quiet the demons that haunted him. Leo missed Priya in ways he hadn't expected. It wasn't just the companionship he craved; it was the intimacy, the warmth of having someone by his side. In his moments of vulnerability, when he lay awake at night staring at the ceiling, he remembered their laughter, their shared dreams, and the way she had looked at him as if he were the only person in the world. Those memories cut deeper than any physical wound, leaving him restless and aching.

One evening, as he left the court after a particularly grueling session, he caught sight of a couple walking hand in hand, their laughter ringing out like music. A pang of envy shot through him, igniting the anger he had tried to suppress. "Why can't I have that?" he thought bitterly. He felt a burning desire to reclaim what he had lost, to prove to himself that he could move on. But every time he attempted to engage with someone new, he found himself retreating, haunted by the specter of Priya.

With the days turning into weeks, Leo made a conscious decision to shift his focus. He would no longer be defined by his heartbreak. Instead, he would throw himself into his career and personal growth. He wanted to become someone who couldn't be rejected, someone who was formidable in his pursuits. The determination took root, a fire igniting within him that pushed him to seek more than just healing. He wanted greatness.

Leo's heart shattered the moment his girlfriend broke up with him. It wasn't a clean break; it was a slow, agonizing unraveling. He replayed every conversation, every argument in his head—trying to pinpoint where things had gone wrong. His mind spiraled, and nights became endless loops of despair. He couldn't sleep, couldn't eat, and nothing could distract him from the black hole that seemed to grow inside him.

The girl he had loved was perfect in his eyes, and in losing her, Leo felt as though he'd lost himself. He spent hours on social media, looking at old photos of them together, torturing himself with memories of happier times. He wondered how she had moved on so easily, while he was left suffocating in his emotions.

It wasn't long before the heartbreak turned to anger—not just at her, but at himself. How could he have let himself be so vulnerable, so dependent on someone else for happiness? He vowed never to let anyone have that kind of power over him again.

The solution to his pain came in the form of tennis, a sport he had once played casually but now embraced with an obsessive fervor. Every swing of the racket, every match was an outlet for his pent-up anger and frustration. He could control his performance on the court, unlike the chaos in his personal life. As his skills sharpened, so did his resolve. The old Leo was gone—replaced by someone who would never be weak again.

Love had made him soft, he believed. From now on, his heart would be impenetrable.

Leo wasn't new to love. Growing up in India, where emotions flowed freely between friends and family, he had been taught that love was everything. It was the bedrock of relationships, the glue that held families together, the spark that turned a mere interaction into something sacred. He had believed in it so wholeheartedly that when it came crashing down, it broke him in ways he hadn't thought possible.

The breakup had come at the worst possible time. It wasn't just the end of a relationship for Leo—it was the end of an era. His teenage years had been spent with her, every milestone punctuated by moments with her at his side. She had been his first everything—his first kiss, his first love, his first heartbreak. They had shared secrets, dreams, and plans for the future. He had imagined growing old with her, building a life together. They had talked about moving away to start fresh in a new city, escaping the expectations of their families. But now, all of that was gone.

Leo lay in bed, staring up at the ceiling, the world a blur around him. It had been months since the breakup, and he hadn't gotten used to the gnawing emptiness that had taken residence inside him. His phone buzzed, but he didn't bother to check it. He knew it wouldn't be her. It hadn't been her in days. She had cut him off completely, leaving him with nothing but memories and questions. He had sent her countless messages, each more desperate than the last, but she never responded. He had tried to call, but every time, his heart would sink a little lower as it went straight to voicemail.

The nights were the worst. They used to talk for hours until they fell asleep on the phone, her soft breathing on the other end a comfort he now longed for. Without her, the silence was deafening. He found himself unable to sleep, replaying every conversation they'd ever had, every argument, every tender moment. He wanted to fix it, to go back and change whatever had caused things to fall apart, but no matter how many times he retraced his steps, he couldn't find the moment when everything had gone wrong.

His friends had tried to help at first. They told him to move on, to distract himself. They suggested nights out, new hobbies, anything to take his mind off of her, but nothing worked. He found himself withdrawing from them, too. Their sympathy irritated him, their encouragement felt hollow. They didn't understand. None of them had ever loved someone the way he had loved her. None of them knew what it was like to feel so completely unmoored, so utterly lost.

In the end, Leo decided he didn't need anyone. Not his friends, not his family, and certainly not her. If love could tear him apart like this, then love wasn't worth it. He wasn't going to let anyone have that kind of power over him ever again. He would focus on himself—on his future, his career, his own goals. He didn't need love. What he needed was success. What he needed was control.

He found his escape on the tennis court. Tennis had been a casual hobby for him, something he enjoyed in his free time, but now it became his obsession. Every time he stepped onto the court, he channeled all of his anger, his frustration, his heartbreak into the game. The sound of the racket hitting the ball became a balm for his wounded soul. With each swing, he released a little more of the pain, a little more of the rage. It was the only thing that made him feel alive anymore.

But tennis wasn't enough to fill the void. He needed something more, something bigger. His career became his new love. If he couldn't have her, he would have success. He would become the best neuroscientist the world had ever seen. He would be so successful, so untouchable, that no one would ever be able to reject him again. He threw himself into his studies with a single-minded focus, pushing himself harder than ever before. Late nights, early mornings, hours spent in the lab—it didn't matter. All that mattered was that he succeeded. And he would. He had to.

Love had failed him, but his ambition would not.

2

THERE IS A DIFFERENT SUN IN INDIA

Months passed, and the ache of heartbreak slowly morphed into a relentless drive for success. Leo had immersed himself in his work, garnering respect from his peers for his dedication and talent. But even as he reached new heights in his career, the void of companionship lingered like a shadow, always present and never truly gone.

It was during a colleague's birthday party that Leo met Mona. She was everything he didn't expect—bold, vivacious, and unapologetically herself. They struck up a conversation over drinks, and Leo found himself captivated by her energy. She exuded confidence, a kind of magnetic charm that drew people in effortlessly. For the first time in a long while, Leo felt a flicker of interest in someone new.

Mona was unlike anyone he had been with before. She wasn't looking for a serious relationship; she was open about her desire for something more casual, something light. Leo was immediately intrigued. He was still a bit broken, still trying to piece his heart back together, and the idea of a fling was enticing. It was a way to distract himself from the lingering thoughts of Priya while indulging in the thrill of attraction.

Their chemistry was undeniable, igniting with every stolen glance and playful exchange. They began meeting at bars and restaurants, their conversations filled with laughter and banter. Leo felt alive again, the laughter washing over him like a balm. With Mona, he could escape the weight of his past and immerse himself in the joy of the present.

One evening, after a particularly exhilarating night out, they found themselves at Leo's apartment, the air thick with anticipation. They kissed passionately, igniting a fire that had been simmering beneath the surface. As the night unfolded, Leo surrendered to the moment, losing himself in the warmth of Mona's embrace. It felt freeing—like shedding the last remnants of his heartbreak and embracing the thrill of something new.

Their fling quickly escalated into a whirlwind romance. Mona was adventurous, dragging Leo along on spontaneous outings—hiking, late-night drives, and beach trips. They created memories together that made Leo forget his heartache, if only for a moment. But as much as he enjoyed the thrill of their encounters, a part of him remained guarded, still haunted by the ghost of Priya.

Mona was clear about her intentions. She wasn't interested in building something long-term. She wanted to enjoy the moment and live life to the fullest. And for Leo, that was refreshing. He didn't need the weight of commitment; he needed freedom, and Mona embodied that.

However, as their time together unfolded, Leo began to realize that he was still affected by his past. He couldn't shake off the moments when he found himself comparing Mona to Priya, wondering if things would have been different had they stayed together. He would catch himself reminiscing about Priya's laughter or the way she had looked at him, and each time, he felt a pang of guilt. It wasn't fair to Mona, who had been nothing but vibrant and supportive.

Despite the fun and excitement, a nagging feeling lingered in the back of his mind. He wanted to fully embrace this new chapter of his life, yet he couldn't completely let go of the emotional baggage. He grappled with the dichotomy of wanting to move on and the memories of what he had lost. Still, he pressed on, using the relationship with Mona as a way to cope.

As weeks turned into months, their relationship flourished, but the specter of Priya lingered like a ghost in the corner of his mind. The moments of passion with Mona were intense, but they were shadowed by fleeting memories that reminded him of a time when love had felt pure and uncomplicated.

One evening, after an adventurous day hiking in the Western Ghats, Leo and Mona returned to his apartment, exhilarated and buzzing with energy. They tumbled onto the couch, their laughter filling the room. As the night wore on, the playful atmosphere shifted, and they found themselves wrapped in each other's arms, the world around them fading away.

But in the stillness that followed, Leo couldn't help but feel an emptiness he hadn't anticipated. Mona's laughter echoed in his ears, yet he felt a void that he couldn't ignore. In that moment, he understood that no matter how much he tried to drown out his feelings, they were still there, lingering beneath the surface.

Despite the intensity of their connection, Leo knew he had to confront his emotions. As the weeks passed, he began to withdraw, pulling back from the relationship. Mona sensed the shift and confronted him one evening, her eyes filled with concern. "Leo, what's going on? You've been distant."

He hesitated, grappling with the words he wanted to say. "I just... I don't think I'm ready for something serious," he finally admitted, his voice barely above a whisper. The honesty felt like a weight lifted off his shoulders, yet it also left him feeling vulnerable.

Mona nodded, her expression softening. "I get it. I just thought we had something special." The disappointment in her eyes cut deep, but Leo knew it was the right decision. They were on different paths, and he needed to prioritize his healing.

As their fling came to an end, Leo felt a mix of relief and sadness. He had experienced a taste of joy and freedom with Mona, yet he was also reminded of the heartache that still lingered within him. It was a bittersweet farewell, but he had to keep moving forward, to keep searching for himself amidst the chaos of emotions.

Leo had lost his friends along the way, isolating himself in his pursuit of success. His days were filled with research and tennis, his nights spent alone, wandering in his mind. Then, one lonely evening, Mona came into his life. She was different from the girl he had loved before—confident, playful, and unattached. What started as a fling quickly spiraled into something more physical. They spent countless nights together—on lonely roads, in hotel rooms, and even in quiet mountain mornings. Each encounter with Mona was another way for Leo to bury his emotions, his past love slowly being replaced by lust.

But Leo's heart wasn't ready for love. It was too bruised, too broken, and soon enough, Mona was just another fleeting chapter in his story.

Leo's transformation was swift. He stopped confiding in his friends, stopped seeking sympathy. They didn't understand the depths of his pain, and their attempts to console him only irritated him further. Slowly, he cut ties with everyone he had once been close to, isolating himself in his pursuit of perfection.

Without the distraction of friendships, Leo threw himself into his studies, channeling every ounce of his energy into his dream of becoming a neuroscientist. His obsession with success replaced the need for emotional connection. He stayed up late, studying the complexities of the human brain, fascinated by how the mind could betray its owner—how love, that elusive chemical reaction, could cause such agony.

Tennis and science became his twin pillars of sanity, but loneliness still crept in during the late hours of the night. That's when Mona came into his life. She wasn't interested in love, which suited Leo perfectly. They met at a party, and after some flirtatious banter, one thing led to another. Their relationship was purely physical, and it was exactly what Leo needed at the time.

Mona became his escape from the emotional numbness. Their nights together were filled with passion—under the stars on deserted roads, in the rain, in hotel rooms. It didn't matter where. It wasn't about connection; it was about filling the void. Leo told himself that this was enough. He didn't need love, didn't need anyone else. But deep down, he knew Mona was just another distraction.

The wolf inside him was still hungry, still searching for something more.

As Leo's transformation progressed, he became colder, more distant. He barely recognized the person he had once been—

the boy who had dreamed of love, who had believed in happy endings. That boy was dead now, buried beneath layers of pain and resentment. In his place was someone else, someone stronger, someone who didn't need anyone else to complete him.

His friends drifted away, sensing the change in him. He no longer called them, no longer joined them for their weekly gatherings. At first, they tried to reach out, but Leo wasn't interested in their sympathy. Their attempts to get him to open up only irritated him. They didn't understand what he was going through. How could they? None of them had ever experienced a love so deep, so consuming. And none of them had felt the kind of pain he was now drowning in.

Isolation became his new normal. Leo didn't mind it, though. He preferred the solitude. It gave him time to focus on his goals, to plan his future. He didn't need friends, didn't need the emotional baggage that came with relationships. What he needed was to prove to the world—and to himself—that he was better off alone.

And then, one night, Mona came into his life.

They met at a party he had reluctantly agreed to attend. It was one of those nights where he had forced himself to be social, to pretend he was fine when he was anything but. He was standing off to the side, nursing a drink he didn't particularly want, when Mona approached him. She was bold, confident, the kind of girl who knew exactly what she wanted and wasn't afraid to go after it. She struck up a conversation, and before he knew it, they were flirting.

For the first time in months, Leo felt a flicker of something—something other than anger or sadness. Mona wasn't like the girl he had loved. She didn't remind him of her, didn't make him think of what he had lost. In fact, she was the exact opposite. Where his ex had been gentle and soft-spoken, Mona was fiery and outspoken. She didn't want love, didn't want commitment. She wanted something else—something simple, something physical.

And that suited Leo just fine.

What started as harmless flirting quickly escalated. They left the party together, and before the night was over, Leo found himself in her bed. It was exhilarating, freeing. For the first time since his breakup, he wasn't thinking about his ex. He wasn't thinking about the past, about what he had lost. He was living in the moment, consumed by the heat of their passion.

Mona became a regular part of Leo's life after that. They didn't talk much about their feelings, didn't discuss what they were or what they wanted. They didn't need to. Their relationship was based on mutual understanding. Neither of them wanted anything serious. They just wanted each other—for now, for the moment. And that was enough.

Their encounters were wild, unpredictable. They would sneak away to deserted roads late at night, their bodies entwined beneath the stars. Sometimes they would meet in hotel rooms, other times in the rain, their clothes soaked as they clung to each other. There were no rules, no expectations. It was raw, primal, and exactly what Leo needed.

But as thrilling as it was, Leo knew deep down that it wasn't enough. Mona was a distraction, a way to numb the pain, but she wasn't the solution. She was just another temporary fix, like tennis or his career. She filled the emptiness for a little while, but once the night was over, the void returned.

Leo told himself it didn't matter. He didn't need more than this. Love had broken him, and he wasn't going to make the same mistake again. He didn't need love. He just needed control.

3

THE SUN RISES BEYOND THE CLOUD

Life moved quickly for Leo. His work brought him to new places, new faces, and new challenges. At his job, he met Bhargi, a stunning woman with a mind as sharp as his. Their first meeting ignited something within him—a magnetic attraction that was both physical and intellectual. Eye contact alone was enough to spark his fantasies.

Their encounters were spontaneous, fueled by desire. Late-night car rides turned into late-night escapades. Cigarettes shared after stolen moments of passion became their ritual. Bhargi wasn't a fling like Mona. She was something more—a dangerous, addictive temptation that pushed Leo deeper into his world of lust.

Leo threw himself back into work after his fling with Mona. He buried himself in research, immersing himself in his projects, trying to forget the emotional turmoil that lingered after their breakup. The neuroscience lab buzzed with activity, and he found solace in the steady rhythm of experiments and data analysis. Each late night spent in the lab was a step further from the remnants of his past.

But life had a way of throwing surprises at him, and soon he found himself face-to-face with Bhargi, a new intern who joined the lab. The moment their eyes met, something clicked. Bhargi had an effortless grace about her, a spark that caught Leo off guard. She was brilliant, with a mind that could unravel complex problems, and her laughter was infectious.

Initially, Leo tried to resist the pull he felt toward her. He was still healing from his past relationships and had sworn off getting involved with anyone new for a while. But the more time he spent with Bhargi, the more he found himself drawn to her. They worked closely on a project, their collaborative efforts leading to late nights in the lab filled with shared ideas and laughter.

One evening, as they wrapped up a successful experiment, Leo invited Bhargi out for dinner. It was a casual outing, but as they talked over plates of steaming food, he found himself captivated by her passion for neuroscience. She spoke with such enthusiasm, her eyes sparkling as she explained her theories. Leo couldn't help but admire her intelligence and dedication.

As they left the restaurant, the city lights twinkling around them, Leo felt a surge of excitement. Bhargi was unlike anyone he had met before; she had a way of making him feel alive, invigorated by their discussions. It was refreshing, and as they walked through the bustling streets, he couldn't shake the feeling that something special was blossoming.

Their connection deepened over the next few weeks, evolving from colleagues to friends. Leo enjoyed their late-night conversations and shared moments, finding comfort in Bhargi's presence. They would often grab coffee in the mornings, discussing everything from their research to their dreams and aspirations. She had a knack for making him laugh, and before long, he realized he had started to let his guard down around her.

One rainy evening, as they sat on the lab's rooftop, watching the rain cascade down the skyline, Leo turned to Bhargi. "You know, I've been through a lot in the past year. I've lost myself a bit," he confessed, his voice soft. "But being around you... it makes me feel like I can find my way back."

Bhargi looked at him, her gaze intense. "Leo, we all go through rough patches. It's how we come out of them that matters. You're stronger than you think." Her words struck a chord within him, igniting a flicker of hope.

As they spent more time together, Leo began to feel something he hadn't felt in a long time—something akin to hope. Bhargi brought light into his life, and he found himself drawn to her, not just as a friend but as something more. The flirtation began subtly, with lingering touches and playful banter that hinted at deeper feelings. Each time their eyes met, he felt the spark igniting, a connection that went beyond the surface.

One evening, after a particularly successful day at work, they found themselves sitting in Bhargi's apartment, sharing a bottle of wine. The conversation flowed easily, laughter filling the space as they reminisced about their shared experiences in the lab. Leo felt a warmth spreading through him, a sense of belonging that he had longed for.

As the night progressed, the air thickened with tension. They sat close on the couch, the space between them charged with unspoken desires. In a moment of boldness, Leo reached for Bhargi's hand, intertwining their fingers. "Can I kiss you?" he asked, his heart racing.

Bhargi smiled, her eyes sparkling with mischief. "I thought you'd never ask." With that, Leo leaned in, capturing her lips in a kiss that felt electric. It was as if the world around them faded away, leaving only the two of them in that moment.

From that night on, their relationship blossomed into a passionate romance. They would steal kisses in the lab, share late-night conversations, and explore the city together. Leo found himself swept away by Bhargi's charm and intelligence, feeling as if he was falling in love for the first time in ages.

But even as he embraced this new chapter, the shadows of his past loomed. The memories of Priya still haunted him, whispering doubts into his ear. Could he truly allow himself to love again? Would he be able to let go of the pain that had once consumed him?

As weeks turned into months, Leo faced the challenge of reconciling his past with his present. He wanted to be with Bhargi, to explore the depths of their connection, but he also feared the vulnerability that came with love. The walls he had built around his heart felt impenetrable at times, and he struggled with the idea of opening up again.

One evening, as they lay together in bed, Leo turned to Bhargi, his heart heavy with uncertainty. "Do you ever think about love?" he asked, his voice barely above a whisper. "I mean, what it really means?"

Bhargi propped herself up on her elbow, her gaze steady. "Love is messy, Leo. It's beautiful and complicated. It requires trust and vulnerability. But it's also worth it," she replied, her expression sincere. "You can't let your past dictate your future. You deserve happiness."

Her words resonated with him, piercing through the layers of fear he had wrapped around himself. In that moment, he realized he couldn't let the fear of heartbreak keep him from experiencing love again. He had to take the leap.

As the weeks went by, Leo opened up more to Bhargi, sharing the scars of his past and the lessons he had learned. Their bond deepened, and he found himself feeling happier than he had in a long time. The warmth of her laughter, the kindness in her eyes, and the thrill of their connection brought him a sense of peace he had longed for.

Leo's career took off. He was becoming known in his field for his sharp intellect and relentless work ethic. But the more he achieved, the less satisfied he felt. His colleagues admired him, but Leo kept them at a distance. He had built walls around his heart so high that no one could breach them—no one, that is, until he met Bhargi.

Bhargi was unlike any woman Leo had met before. She was ambitious, intelligent, and strikingly beautiful. There was an intensity in her gaze that caught Leo off guard, and for the first time in a long while, he felt a flicker of something beyond lust. It wasn't love, not yet—but it was something that intrigued him.

Their first interaction was brief but electric. A glance, a smile, and suddenly, Leo found himself thinking about her in ways he hadn't thought about anyone since his ex. He imagined what it would be like to be with her, not just physically, but intellectually. There was a fire in her that mirrored his own, and it drew him in.

Their relationship unfolded quickly. Late nights at the office turned into car rides where their attraction boiled over into something primal. They shared cigarettes after their moments together, their conversations laced with the thrill of the forbidden. Bhargi was dangerous—someone who could challenge him, who could keep up with him. But Leo wasn't looking for something serious. He wasn't ready to be vulnerable again.

Bhargi was another chapter in his journey—another piece of his puzzle.

Leo had always been ambitious, but after the breakup, his career became his sole focus. He wasn't just driven—he was obsessed. His research in neuroscience consumed him. Every waking moment was spent working, thinking, planning. He was determined to be the best, to rise to the top of his field. He would become so successful that no one—especially not his ex—could ever look down on him again.

It was during this intense period of focus that he met Bhargi. She worked in the same research department as him, and from the moment they crossed paths, Leo felt something shift. Bhargi was stunning—confident, intelligent, and completely captivating. There was an air of mystery about her, something that drew Leo in despite himself.

Their first meeting was brief, just a passing exchange in the hallway, but Leo couldn't stop thinking about her afterward. There was something in her eyes, something that ignited a spark in him that he hadn't felt in a long time. He tried to push the thoughts away, tried to focus on his work, but Bhargi lingered in his mind like a distant flame.

As fate would have it, they were assigned to work on a project together. It was an opportunity for Leo to get to know her better, and before long, the professional boundaries between them began to blur. Late nights in the lab turned into long conversations, and those conversations soon became something more. There was an unspoken tension between them, an attraction that neither of them could deny.

It wasn't long before that tension exploded into something physical. One night, after an especially stressful day, Leo offered to give Bhargi a ride home. The drive was quiet at first, the city lights flickering past as they made their way through the darkened streets. But when they reached her apartment, neither of them made a move to get out. Instead, they sat there in the car, the silence between them thick with unspoken desire.

And then, without a word, Bhargi leaned in and kissed him.

The kiss was sudden, but it was electric. Leo felt the surge of adrenaline course through his veins, his heart pounding in his chest. For a brief moment, the chaos of his life seemed to disappear, drowned out by the intensity of Bhargi's lips on his. It wasn't soft or tender, like kisses he had known before. It was urgent, desperate, the kind of kiss that blurred the line between lust and something darker.

Without a word, they moved to the back seat of the car, their bodies tangled in the confined space, the heat of their desire burning through the cool night air. The windows fogged up as their hands explored each other, and soon, they were lost in a frenzy of passion that neither of them could control. It was raw and primal, an act of release as much as it was a connection between two people.

When it was over, they sat in the silence of the car, both of them catching their breath. Bhargi's hair was tousled, her eyes still burning with the intensity of what had just happened. Leo leaned back against the seat, his mind racing. He didn't feel the guilt he thought he might. Instead, he felt something else— something more dangerous. He felt power. Bhargi was different from the other women in his life, and he liked it. She wasn't just a distraction; she was a challenge.

Over the next few weeks, Leo and Bhargi's encounters became more frequent. They kept their relationship hidden, sneaking away from the office at odd hours to steal moments of passion.

Sometimes it was in his car after a long day at work, other times in her apartment, where they'd share a cigarette after sex, their bodies still warm from the heat of their connection.

But for Leo, it wasn't just about the physical. Bhargi ignited something in him that he hadn't felt in a long time. She was intelligent, confident, and fiercely independent—everything he admired. Yet there was also a darkness in her, a fire that matched his own. She didn't ask for love, didn't need his promises or his heart. Like Mona, she wanted something more primal. But unlike Mona, Bhargi's hold on him wasn't fleeting. She became an obsession.

Leo found himself thinking about her constantly. Every time they locked eyes across the office, his mind would wander to the things they'd done together, the moments they shared. It wasn't love, but it was intoxicating, and Leo couldn't get enough. She became his escape from the stress of his work, from the emotional wreckage that still lingered in the corners of his mind.

Yet, as their relationship deepened, Leo couldn't shake the feeling that he was playing with fire. Bhargi wasn't like the other women he had been with. She had power—real power. She knew exactly what she wanted, and she didn't play by the rules. And the more Leo got to know her, the more he realized that she wasn't just a fleeting affair. She was someone who could change him, someone who could pull him further down the path he was already walking.

But Leo didn't care. He was already too far gone. He wanted her. And as long as she was in his life, he would take whatever she gave him.

But just as things began to feel perfect, fate intervened once more. Leo received news of a transfer to Bangalore, an opportunity that could advance his career significantly. It was a chance he couldn't pass up, but it also meant leaving behind the life he had started to build with Bhargi.

The news hit him hard. The thought of leaving her felt unbearable, and he wrestled with the decision. He wanted to take the leap for his career, but could he walk away from the love he had finally allowed himself to embrace?

After a sleepless night, he decided to talk to Bhargi. He wanted to be honest about the opportunity and how it would affect them. "I got a transfer to Bangalore," he said, his voice heavy with emotion. "It's a big opportunity for me, but I don't want to lose what we have."

Bhargi looked at him, her expression a mixture of surprise and understanding. "Leo, this is your dream. You have to go for it. But that doesn't mean we have to end things. We can make this work."

Her response surprised him. He had expected her to be upset, but instead, she was supportive and encouraging. They discussed how they could maintain their relationship despite the distance, and Leo felt a renewed sense of hope. They made plans to visit each other regularly, to continue nurturing their bond, no matter the miles between them.

With that decision, Leo packed his bags and headed to Bangalore, determined to succeed in both his career and his relationship with Bhargi. He was ready to embrace the challenges that lay ahead, knowing that he had someone worth fighting for on the other side.

4

THE BANGALORE CONNECTION

Bangalore welcomed Leo with its lush greenery and vibrant tech culture. The transition from the bustling streets of Mumbai to the quieter, more laid-back atmosphere of Bangalore was a breath of fresh air. He settled into his new job at the research facility, diving headfirst into his work. Each day presented new challenges and opportunities for growth, and Leo relished the chance to prove himself.

But as the weeks went by, he found himself missing Bhargi more than he anticipated. The phone calls and video chats kept them connected, but nothing could replace the intimacy of being physically present with someone you cared for. He often thought about their late-night talks and stolen kisses, and it left a void that felt increasingly difficult to fill.

Leo's career continued to rise, and with it came a transfer to Bangalore. It was in this bustling city that Leo found another temporary solace in the form of Rita. She was bold and unapologetic, and their time together painted Bangalore red—literally. Their relationship was fiery and raw, a perfect outlet for the intense emotions that Leo carried within him.

When Leo got transferred to Bangalore, he embraced the change with open arms. The city was vibrant, full of new opportunities and new distractions. Rita entered his life shortly after his move. She was fierce, unfiltered, and unapologetically herself. She wasn't looking for anything permanent either, which made her perfect for Leo.

Their relationship was fiery, passionate, and all-consuming. With Rita, there were no strings attached, no promises made. They spent nights together exploring the city, their time spent in a haze of lust and excitement. For Leo, Bangalore became a playground where he could indulge in his desires without consequence. He told himself that this was freedom—that this was what he had always wanted.

Life had taken on a chaotic rhythm for Leo. His career was advancing at a rapid pace, and he was gaining recognition for his work in neuroscience. His days were filled with research, his nights a blur of physical encounters with Bhargi and the occasional rendezvous with Mona. It was an unsustainable cycle, but Leo didn't care. The more he threw himself into his work and his lust, the less he had to think about the emptiness that still gnawed at his soul.

That was, until the transfer to Bangalore came through.

Rita She was different from Mona and Bhargi—her beauty was more understated, but there was an undeniable spark in her eyes. They met at a networking event for professionals, where Rita worked in a field adjacent to neuroscience. From the moment they struck up a conversation, Leo was captivated by her sharp wit and bold attitude. She wasn't afraid to challenge him, to push back on his ideas, and that intrigued him more than anything.

As the night wore on, they found themselves standing on the rooftop of the event venue, the city lights twinkling beneath them. Leo felt an attraction building between them, and Rita didn't shy away from it. They talked for hours, but the tension between them was palpable. And when she finally leaned in to kiss him, Leo didn't hesitate.

Bangalore became a new playground for Leo's increasingly reckless desires. He and Rita would meet in secret, their passion igniting like wildfire. Unlike his encounters with Mona and Bhargi, his time with Rita was more intense, more all-consuming. She pushed him to his limits, both physically and mentally, and Leo found himself lost in her. With every kiss, every touch, the world around them faded away, leaving only the heat of their connection.

But Rita wasn't just a fling. She became Leo's anchor in the city, someone who understood him on a level that others didn't. She didn't ask for commitment or promises, but there was an unspoken bond between them, a sense of belonging. For a while, Leo thought that maybe—just maybe—Rita could be the one to fill the void that still haunted him.

But then came Rachel.

Bangalore was a city of contrasts—modern yet traditional, bustling yet serene. It was a place where ambition thrived, and for Leo, it was an opportunity to take his career to the next level. His transfer to a prestigious neuroscience institute in the city was everything he had worked for, but it also meant leaving behind the life he had built. Mona, Bhargi, and the tangled mess of emotions that came with them—it was time to leave them in the past. Or so he thought.

But Bangalore wasn't just Rita's city. On his tennis match days, Leo encountered Rachael, a divorced mother with a seductive allure. Rachael's touch seemed to fuel his performance on the court, and their nights together were filled with a passion he had never experienced before. Rachael's life was messy, but in her arms, Leo found something he couldn't quite define. For a moment, it felt like everything had a purpose.

Despite their differences, there was an undeniable chemistry between them. Their relationship was different from anything Leo had experienced before. With Rachael, there was a depth to their connection that went beyond physical attraction.

Rachael made Leo feel alive in ways he hadn't felt since his ex. Their nights together were filled with laughter, deep conversations, and a passion that bordered on something more profound. But Leo kept his distance emotionally. He couldn't afford to get attached, not when he had spent so long building up his defenses.

Rachael gave him something he hadn't realized he needed—a sense of grounding. But Leo knew better than to let himself fall. He had learned his lesson the hard way, and he wasn't about to make the same mistake again.

It was during one of his lunch breaks at the lab that he met Rita. She was a researcher from another department, and they had crossed paths at a seminar. Rita was intriguing, with a fierce intellect and a refreshing outlook on life. Their conversations flowed effortlessly, and before long, they were spending more time together.

At first, Leo was hesitant. He didn't want to jeopardize his relationship with Bhargi, but there was something magnetic about Rita that pulled him in. She was adventurous and had a carefree spirit that reminded him of his own desire to break free from the constraints of his past. They began to hang out more, exploring the city together, visiting cafes, and attending events. The chemistry was undeniable, and Leo found himself drawn to her.

One evening, after a particularly fun night out, they returned to Rita's apartment, the atmosphere charged with excitement. The tension between them was palpable, and as they sat on the couch, Leo felt the weight of his choices pressing down on him.

Should he risk it all for a fling, or should he remain loyal to Bhargi?

As they talked, the conversation shifted to their aspirations and dreams. Rita shared her ambitions and how she wanted to make a mark in the research community. Her passion was contagious, and Leo felt invigorated by her words. In that moment, the barriers he had built around himself began to crumble, and he surrendered to the moment.

One kiss led to another, and soon they were wrapped in each other's arms, the world outside fading away. It was exhilarating, and Leo found himself lost in the thrill of the moment. The connection they shared was intense, fueled by their shared passions and the excitement of new beginnings.

However, as the days turned into weeks, Leo found himself caught in a whirlwind of emotions. His fling with Rita was exhilarating, yet it was clouded by guilt. He knew he had crossed a line, and every time he spoke to Bhargi, he felt a pang of remorse. It wasn't fair to her, and he grappled with the implications of his actions.

As his relationship with Rita blossomed, so did his internal conflict. He enjoyed the excitement and adventure she brought into his life, yet a part of him longed for the depth of connection he had with Bhargi. He found himself torn between the thrill of new love and the stability of a relationship that felt like home.

In the back of his mind, Leo knew he had to confront his feelings. He had to decide what he truly wanted. He began to reflect on his relationship with Bhargi, weighing the warmth of their connection against the fiery passion he shared with Rita. It was a tug-of-war within his heart, and he struggled to find clarity.

One afternoon, as he sat in a park, he received a call from Bhargi. Her voice was warm and familiar, and as they spoke, he felt the familiar comfort of their bond. They discussed their lives, their aspirations, and the challenges of distance. Bhargi's support was unwavering, and it made Leo realize just how much she meant to him.

That evening, after the call, Leo found himself lying in bed, staring at the ceiling. The weight of his decisions hung heavily on his chest. He knew he had to make a choice, to confront the consequences of his actions. He couldn't keep living in a state of uncertainty, juggling two relationships.

Leo decided to take a step back from Rita. He needed to clarify his feelings and ensure that he was not leading anyone on. He met Rita at a café, the atmosphere charged with unspoken words. As they sat across from each other, he felt a mixture of excitement and apprehension.

"Rita, I need to be honest with you," he began, his voice steady. "I've been seeing someone else. I didn't intend for this to happen, but I can't continue to juggle both of you."

Rita's expression shifted, surprise flickering in her eyes. "I appreciate your honesty, Leo. I thought we had something real, but I understand." Her voice was steady, but Leo could see the disappointment etched on her face.

"I really enjoyed our time together," he continued, regret filling his heart. "But I can't betray Bhargi. She means a lot to me."

Rita nodded, her gaze unwavering. "I get it. We had a spark, but I respect your decision." As they parted ways, Leo felt a mix of relief and sadness. He had made the right choice, but it didn't erase the thrill of what they had shared.

As Leo settled back into his routine, he focused on his work and tried to maintain a connection with Bhargi. The distance was still challenging, but he was determined to make it work. He knew he had to put in the effort, to nurture the bond they had built despite the miles between them.

5

LET'S GO TO LONDON

The time came for Leo to take the next step in his career, and he was presented with an incredible opportunity to work in London. It was a dream come true, a chance to advance his research and make a mark in the field of neuroscience. But the excitement of the move was overshadowed by the reality of leaving behind everything he had built in Bangalore.

As Leo's career progressed, he received an opportunity to move to London. It was a fresh start, a chance to leave behind the flings, the chaos, and the weight of his past. But before he left, he made sure that his connections with Mona, Bhargi, Rita, and Rachael ended in ways they would never forget. Each of them was left with a memory, a piece of Leo that he hoped would keep him in their minds long after he had gone.

On his flight to London, Leo met a girl from Delhi. The conversation flowed easily between them, and Leo couldn't help but feel his old charm creeping back. He knew how to make her fall for him, but his attention was quickly diverted. Sabar, his mentor in London, had arranged for someone to meet him at the airport, and in the turbulence of the flight, fate intervened.

It was the fresh start he needed, a chance to leave behind the women, the chaos, and the distractions that had defined his life for the past few years. Before he left, he made sure to end things with each of the women in his life—Rita, Rachael, Bhargi, and Mona. He wasn't cruel about it, but he was firm. They had all been important to him in their own way, but they were part of a chapter he was closing.

On his flight to London, Leo sat next to a girl from Delhi. She was charming, witty, and full of life. Their conversation flowed easily, and for the first time in a while, Leo felt his old charisma returning. He could make her fall for him if he wanted to, but that wasn't his goal. His mind was already focused on London, where Sabar, his mentor, awaited him.

Sabar had been instrumental in guiding Leo's career path, helping him secure the position in London. But it wasn't just the job that awaited him—Sabar had something else in store for Leo, something that would change the course of his life forever.

As Leo boarded the plane to London, he felt a mix of anticipation and anxiety. He was leaving behind Bhargi, and even though they had agreed to continue their relationship, the uncertainty loomed large. He couldn't shake off the feeling that their bond would be tested in ways he couldn't predict.

Settling into his seat, Leo gazed out the window, watching as the cityscape of Bangalore faded into the distance. His mind drifted back to Bhargi, the laughter they had shared, and the moments of vulnerability that had brought them closer. He had committed to making things work, but the thought of navigating a long-distance relationship filled him with apprehension.

As the plane ascended, Leo felt a surge of excitement. London was a city brimming with possibilities, and he was ready to embrace it. The thought of exploring the vibrant culture, meeting new people, and diving into his work filled him with optimism. He envisioned the opportunities that awaited him, the breakthroughs he could achieve in his research.

They spent the rest of the flight catching up, reminiscing about their childhood and sharing stories of where life had taken them since they had last seen each other. Leo felt a warmth in his chest that he hadn't experienced in years. There was something about Sharmi that brought him back to a simpler time—a time when love wasn't complicated by lust or fleeting desires.

As they talked, Leo found himself opening up to Sharmi in a way he hadn't with anyone in years. He told her about the heartbreak that had changed him, the flings that had left him feeling hollow, and the anger he had poured into his career and sports. To his surprise, Sharmi didn't judge him. She listened with empathy, her eyes reflecting understanding and compassion.

"I think we all go through phases where we're searching for something," Sharmi said softly. "But sometimes what we're searching for is already within us."

Her words struck a chord with Leo. He had been searching for fulfillment in all the wrong places—through his flings, his career, and even his anger. But sitting next to Sharmi, he realized that what he had been missing all along was love—the kind of love that was genuine, unselfish, and deep.

As the plane began its descent into London, Leo felt a sense of clarity he hadn't experienced in years. Sharmi was the missing piece, the person who had reminded him of the kind of love he had once believed in.

When they landed, Leo walked with Sharmi through the airport, his heart racing with the possibility of what could be. But as they reached the terminal, reality hit him. Sharmi was in London for only a short time, and they were both on different paths. Still, the connection they had rekindled was undeniable.

"I'm glad we reconnected, Leo," Sharmi said as they prepared to part ways. "But I don't know what the future holds."

Neither did Leo, but for the first time in years, he felt hopeful. "I don't either, but I'd like to find out," he replied.

Sharmi smiled and hugged him tightly, her embrace sending waves of warmth through his body. "Take care of yourself, Leo," she whispered.

And with that, she was gone, disappearing into the bustling crowd of the airport.

Over the next few months in London, Leo couldn't stop thinking about Sharmi. She had left an indelible mark on his heart, one that no fling or casual encounter could ever erase.

But despite his longing to reconnect with her, life had a way of keeping them apart. Sharmi was busy with her own work and travels, and Leo's career demanded much of his time.

Still, he held onto the hope that fate would bring them together again.

As the year passed, Leo threw himself into his work, determined to succeed as a neuroscientist. His career flourished, and he found satisfaction in his achievements, but there was always a part of him that felt incomplete without Sharmi. The fleeting connections he made with others paled in comparison to the deep bond he had shared with her.

Then, one fateful evening, after almost a year of silence, Leo received a message from Sharmi. She was back in London, and she wanted to meet.

Mid-flight, Leo decided to strike up a conversation with the woman sitting next to him. She was from Delhi, and they quickly bonded over their shared love for travel and ambition. Her name was Aisha, and she was heading to London for work as well. They exchanged stories and laughter, the conversation flowing effortlessly between them.

Aisha was captivating—her confidence and zest for life infectious. As they talked, Leo felt a flicker of connection that reminded him of the excitement he had felt with both Mona and Rita. But he also felt a pang of guilt; he was still committed to Bhargi, and he didn't want to lead Aisha on.

After hours of engaging conversation, they exchanged numbers, agreeing to meet up once they arrived in London. Leo felt a mixture of excitement and hesitation. The connection was undeniable, but he had to tread carefully. He didn't want to jeopardize the relationship he had started to build with Bhargi.

For a moment, Leo even found himself enjoying her company, forgetting about the emotional wreckage he had left behind.

But as the plane hit a bout of turbulence, Leo's thoughts took a darker turn. His stomach lurched, and suddenly, the calm exterior he had been trying to maintain cracked. He excused himself and made his way toward the emergency exit, needing to clear his head. The world around him seemed to blur as memories of his past came rushing back—the breakup, the anger, the countless women who had crossed his path since.

And that's when he saw her.

Standing near the emergency exit, with her back turned, was Sharmi.

Leo's heart stopped. It couldn't be. Sharmi was part of a past he had buried deep, a love he thought he would never see again. But there she was, as real as the turbulence shaking the plane. Her long, dark hair cascaded down her back, just as he remembered it, and in that moment, all of the anger and lust that had been driving him seemed to evaporate. He hadn't realized how much he had missed her until now.

Leo stood frozen for what felt like an eternity, torn between disbelief and an overwhelming desire to speak to her. His feet moved almost on their own, bringing him closer to her. When she finally turned around, their eyes met, and the connection between them was immediate—electric. It was as if the years apart hadn't changed anything.

"Sharmi?" Leo's voice was barely above a whisper, but she heard him.

She didn't say anything at first. Instead, she stepped closer and wrapped her arms around him, pulling him into a tight embrace. For the first time in what felt like forever, Leo felt warmth. Real warmth. Not the heat of passion, not the fire of lust, but the kind of warmth that only comes from being truly seen and understood.

In that moment, everything else faded away. The pain, the anger, the flings—they all dissolved into nothing. Sharmi's embrace was all that mattered. His heart, which had been hardened by heartbreak and betrayal, softened in her arms. He could feel the years of resentment melting away as she held him, and for the first time in a long time, he felt like he could breathe.

Upon landing in London, Leo was greeted by a bustling airport filled with people from all walks of life. The energy was exhilarating, and as he navigated through the terminals, he felt a sense of freedom that he hadn't experienced in a long time. This was a new beginning, a chance to reinvent himself and pursue his dreams.

As he exited the airport, he was met by Sabar, his mentor and guide in London. Sabar had been a pillar of support during Leo's transition, and as they drove through the city, he shared insights about the research community and the exciting projects Leo could be a part of.

But amidst the discussions of work and ambition, Leo's mind drifted back to Aisha. He knew he had to keep things platonic, but the chemistry they had shared on the flight lingered in the back of his mind. He wanted to explore the city with her, but he also wanted to honor the commitment he had made to Bhargi.

That evening, Leo settled into his new apartment, the excitement of London settling in. He unpacked his belongings, organizing his space in a way that felt familiar yet new. As he prepared for bed, his phone buzzed with a message from Aisha.

"Hey! Let's meet tomorrow and explore the city together. I'm excited to show you around!" Her enthusiasm was infectious, and Leo couldn't help but smile. He agreed, but a part of him felt the weight of his commitment to Bhargi pressing down.

The next day, Leo met Aisha at a café in the heart of London. They wandered through the streets, soaking in the sights and sounds, their laughter echoing in the crisp air. Aisha was vivacious, her love for life shining through in every interaction. They explored iconic landmarks, sharing stories and dreams, and Leo found himself swept up in the excitement of their connection.

But as the day unfolded, Leo couldn't shake the feeling of guilt that lingered in the back of his mind. He kept thinking about

Bhargi, about the bond they had built and the promise he had made to stay committed. It wasn't fair to Aisha to engage in something that could lead to complications.

As the sun began to set, casting a warm glow over the city, they found themselves sitting on a bench near the Thames River. Aisha turned to Leo, her expression serious. "You know, it's refreshing to meet someone who's passionate about their work. I feel like we have a connection, and I'd love to get to know you better."

Leo felt a mix of emotions swirling within him. Aisha was captivating, and he enjoyed their time together, but he also knew he had to be honest. "Aisha, I really enjoy spending time with you, but I need to be upfront. I'm in a committed relationship with someone back in India," he admitted, his heart racing.

Aisha's expression shifted, but she maintained her composure. "I appreciate your honesty, Leo. It's rare to find someone who values commitment." They shared a moment of silence, the weight of their unspoken feelings hanging in the air.

The rest of the evening felt bittersweet. Leo knew he had made the right choice, but the connection he felt with Aisha lingered in the back of his mind. He returned home that night, his heart heavy with the realization that navigating relationships was more complex than he had anticipated.

As the days turned into weeks, Leo focused on his work in London, pouring his energy into research and immersing himself in the vibrant community. He kept in touch with Bhargi, and their late-night video calls became a cherished routine. They shared their successes, their struggles, and the little moments that made life beautiful.

But Aisha remained a constant presence in his thoughts. They had become friends, and Leo appreciated their connection, but he was determined to keep things platonic. He valued Bhargi too much to jeopardize their relationship, even as the allure of Aisha's energy and vivacity lingered.

One afternoon, while working in the lab, Leo received a message from Aisha, inviting him to an art exhibition that evening. He hesitated, torn between his desire to support her and his commitment to Bhargi. After a moment of contemplation, he decided to go, knowing that he could keep things friendly.

At the exhibition, Leo marveled at the creativity and talent on display. Aisha was radiant, her excitement infectious as she guided him through the various exhibits. They laughed, shared insights about the art, and Leo felt a sense of ease in her presence.

But as the night progressed, he could sense the tension between them shifting. Aisha's playful demeanor began to blur the lines, and Leo felt the pull of attraction intensifying. It scared him; he didn't want to hurt Bhargi, but he also couldn't deny the chemistry he felt with Aisha.

In a moment of spontaneity, Aisha leaned in closer, brushing her hand against Leo's. "You know, I really enjoy being around you," she said softly, her gaze searching his. "I feel like we have something special."

Leo's heart raced. He was torn between the thrill of the moment and the weight of his commitment. He leaned back slightly, taking a breath to steady himself. "Aisha, I think you're amazing, but I need you to understand that I'm with someone else. I don't want to cross that line."

Aisha nodded, her expression thoughtful. "I respect that, Leo. It's just hard to ignore the connection we have. But I won't push it." They continued to enjoy the exhibition, but the tension lingered, leaving Leo feeling unsettled.

As the night drew to a close, he left the exhibition feeling conflicted. He appreciated Aisha's understanding, but he couldn't shake the feeling of temptation that lingered. He needed to clarify his feelings and commit fully to the path he had chosen with Bhargi.

That night, as he lay in bed, he reflected on his journey. He had come a long way, navigating the complexities of relationships, and he knew he had to remain true to himself. Bhargi deserved his honesty and commitment, and he didn't want to jeopardize the love they had built.

6

LONDON FOG THE LONG-DISTANCE LOVE

As the months passed, Leo settled into his new life in London, balancing the demands of work and maintaining a long-distance relationship with Bhargi. Their late-night video calls had become a lifeline, a bridge that connected them despite the miles. They shared their experiences, dreams, and everyday moments, cherishing the bond they had built.

Yet, as time went on, Leo began to feel the strain of distance. The longing for Bhargi was palpable, and he found himself missing her presence in ways he hadn't anticipated. The late-night conversations provided comfort, but he yearned for the intimacy of being together.

One evening, as they spoke over video chat, Leo noticed a hint of sadness in Bhargi's eyes. "I miss you, Leo," she said softly. "It's hard not being able to see you in person."

"I miss you too," he replied, his heart aching at the thought of their separation. "I wish I could be there with you."

They discussed their plans for the future, their hopes to bridge the distance, but Leo couldn't shake the feeling of uncertainty that lingered. The challenges of a long-distance relationship were becoming more apparent, and he wondered if they could sustain the connection over time.

Around the same time, Aisha became a more significant presence in Leo's life. They continued to spend time together, attending events, exploring the city, and engaging in deep conversations about their aspirations. Aisha's vibrant personality was invigorating, and Leo found solace in her friendship. But with each passing day, he felt the boundaries between friendship and something more begin to blur.

One afternoon, while they were working on a project together, Aisha turned to Leo, her expression earnest. "I know you're in a relationship, but I can't help but feel like there's something between us," she said softly. "I don't want to complicate things for you, but I have to be honest."

Leo felt a rush of conflicting emotions. He appreciated Aisha's honesty, but it left him feeling trapped. "Aisha, I care about you, but I'm committed to Bhargi. I don't want to hurt her or jeopardize what we have," he replied firmly.

"I get it," Aisha said, her voice tinged with disappointment. "But I want you to know that I'm here if you ever want to talk." Leo appreciated her understanding, but the weight of his feelings began to feel heavier. He was caught in a delicate balance between two worlds, and it was becoming increasingly difficult to navigate.

As Leo continued to work in London, the pressure mounted. The demands of his job intensified, and he found himself pouring more hours into research, using work as an escape from his emotional turmoil. The distance from Bhargi felt more pronounced, and he struggled to maintain the connection they had.

Despite the challenges, Leo remained committed to Bhargi. He wanted to be the partner she deserved, but the temptation of Aisha lingered in his mind. The moments they shared were exciting, and he often found himself thinking about the potential of a different kind of connection.

One night, after a particularly challenging day at work, Leo found himself alone in his apartment, feeling the weight of his choices. He picked up the phone and called Bhargi, desperate for her familiar voice. As they spoke, he felt the comfort of her presence, but he also sensed her concern.

"Leo, are you okay?" Bhargi asked, her voice laced with worry. "You seem distant."

"I'm just busy with work," he replied, trying to sound casual, but the truth was that he felt torn. "It's been a lot to handle, but I'm managing."

Bhargi paused, her gaze penetrating. "You know you can talk to me about anything, right? I'm here for you, no matter the distance." Her words filled him with warmth, but they also amplified his guilt. He didn't want to burden her with the complexity of his feelings.

In the following weeks, Leo tried to focus on his relationship with Bhargi, but the distance weighed heavily on him. The longing for her presence and the thrill of new possibilities created a storm of confusion within him. He began to realize that he couldn't keep living in this limbo forever.

Determined to clarify his feelings, Leo reached out to Aisha. They met at a cozy café, and he decided to be straightforward. "Aisha, I need to be honest with you. I'm struggling with the situation. I value our friendship, but I can't ignore the fact that I'm in a committed relationship."

Aisha listened attentively, her expression calm. "I appreciate your honesty, Leo. I care about you, but I also respect your commitment. If we're going to maintain our friendship, we need to establish some boundaries." Leo nodded, feeling a sense of relief wash over him. They discussed how they could remain friends while respecting the boundaries of his relationship with Bhargi.

After their conversation, Leo felt lighter, as if a weight had been lifted. He realized he needed to commit fully to Bhargi, to invest in their relationship and nurture their bond. He began to make plans for a visit back to India, determined to reconnect and reignite the spark they had.

As Leo prepared for his trip, he felt a surge of excitement. He couldn't wait to see Bhargi, to hold her in his arms and remind her of how much she meant to him. The distance had tested their relationship, but he was ready to face the challenge head-on.

The moment Leo stepped off the plane in India, a wave of nostalgia washed over him. The familiar sights and sounds enveloped him, and he felt a rush of warmth as he navigated through the bustling airport. He couldn't wait to see Bhargi, to finally close the distance that had kept them apart for so long.

When he arrived at her apartment, Bhargi greeted him with open arms. They embraced tightly, the distance between them melting away in an instant. As they pulled back, their eyes met, and Leo felt a wave of emotions flooding through him. "I missed you," he said, his voice filled with sincerity.

"I missed you too," Bhargi replied, her eyes sparkling with joy. They spent the next few days rediscovering each other, sharing laughter, stories, and dreams. Leo felt a renewed sense of love for her, and it reminded him of why he had committed to their relationship in the first place.

As they explored the city together, Leo couldn't help but notice how much he had missed Bhargi's presence. She was his anchor, and being with her felt like coming home. They shared intimate moments, rekindling the spark that had been dimmed by distance.

One evening, as they strolled along a quiet street, Leo turned to Bhargi, his heart racing. "I want you to know that I'm all in. I'm committed to us, no matter the distance," he said earnestly.

Bhargi's expression softened, and she took his hand. "I want that too, Leo. I believe we can make this work." They shared a kiss under the starry sky, the warmth of their connection enveloping them.

Leo's first few weeks in London were a blur of new experiences. The city was massive, full of energy and possibilities. But amidst the excitement, there was an emptiness inside him. He missed something—or someone—and he didn't know what it was until he met Sharmi.

Sharmi wasn't just another woman in his life. She was *the* woman. The moment their eyes met, Leo knew he had found what he had been searching for all along. She wasn't like the others. She was warm, gentle, and everything he had lost sight of during his journey of self-destruction. In Sharmi, he saw the innocence and love he had once believed in.

They talked about their childhoods, reminiscing about simpler times. It was as though they had known each other in another life. Sharmi's presence made Leo feel alive again, but it also made him realize how lost he had been. The anger, the flings, the lust—it all seemed meaningless now.

But Sharmi was not an easy prize to win. She was cautious, and their circumstances made it difficult for them to be together. Leo's career demanded his attention, and their lives pulled them in different directions. For a year, Leo lived without seeing her, but the thought of Sharmi stayed with him, lingering in the back of his mind, keeping his heart anchored to something real.

As Leo returned to London, he felt rejuvenated and filled with hope. He was determined to continue nurturing his relationship with Bhargi, to invest in their future together. The challenges of distance were still present, but he was ready to face them head-on, knowing that their love could withstand the trials ahead.

But love, Leo knew all too well, was never that simple.

Sharmi's presence in his life felt like a miracle, but as quickly as she had reappeared, she was gone. The turbulence passed, the plane steadied, and Sharmi returned to her seat. They exchanged phone numbers before they parted ways at the airport, but life in London was chaotic, and weeks turned into months without any word from her.

Leo threw himself back into his work, but the fire that had driven him in Bangalore wasn't the same. Sharmi had reignited something in him—something he thought he had lost for good. He missed her in a way that made everything else seem pointless. His flings with women like Bhargi and Rita had been distractions, but now that he had seen Sharmi again, the void they had filled felt deeper.

Despite the brief contact with her, Leo's life in London moved forward at an unstoppable pace. He was making significant strides in his research, his colleagues respected him, and his reputation was growing. But he couldn't shake the feeling that something was missing. And in his loneliness, the wolf inside him began to resurface.

The first few months in London were a whirlwind of work and occasional flings. Leo met women through his research institute, at bars, even during weekend tennis matches. None of them meant anything to him, but they filled the emptiness when the nights became too long to bear. Each woman was another conquest, another body to distract him from the thoughts of Sharmi.

Then there was Sabar.

Sabar was introduced to Leo through a mutual friend, a guide of sorts for Leo's professional ambitions in London. She was older than him, a successful woman who had made her mark in the corporate world. Sabar became both a mentor and a companion in his life, showing him the ropes of London while encouraging his professional growth.

But Sabar wasn't just a mentor. She was a temptation. From their very first meeting, there was a simmering attraction between them. Sabar was magnetic—confident, powerful, the kind of woman who commanded respect wherever she went. She pushed Leo to be better, to aim higher, and he found himself drawn to her in ways he hadn't expected.

They started spending more time together, meeting for drinks after work, having dinner at upscale restaurants. Sabar introduced Leo to a world of wealth and sophistication that he hadn't known before, and he found himself getting lost in it. There was an intensity to their relationship, a fire that burned between them. It wasn't love, but it was thrilling.

One night, after a particularly intense work meeting, Sabar invited Leo back to her penthouse. The invitation was clear—

there was no need for words. Leo knew where the night was headed, and he didn't hesitate.

But as they stood on the balcony of her penthouse, looking out at the glittering city below, Leo's thoughts drifted back to Sharmi. Sabar was everything he had wanted after his heartbreak—successful, independent, unattached. But Sharmi... Sharmi had been something else. She had been the one who made him feel alive again, who made him remember what it was like to love.

And yet, Sharmi was nowhere to be found.

The night with Sabar was electric, but when it was over, Leo felt nothing. The wolf inside him was growing tired. He was starting to realize that no amount of success, no number of flings, would ever fill the void that Sharmi had left in his heart.

7

WINTER NIGHTS IN LONDON THE CROSSROADS OF COMMITMENT

In the months that followed, Leo's commitment to Bhargi deepened as he focused on making their long-distance relationship work. They set regular video calls, planned visits, and discussed their future together. Each conversation reinforced their bond, reminding Leo of the love that had blossomed between them.

However, life in London continued to challenge him in unexpected ways. Aisha remained a close friend, and while Leo maintained boundaries, the chemistry between them occasionally sparked moments of tension. Aisha was understanding, yet he could sense her growing frustration with the limitations of their friendship.

One evening, Leo and Aisha met for dinner to discuss their research project. As they sat across from each other in a cozy restaurant, he noticed the way her laughter filled the air, a reminder of the connection they had forged. But as the night wore on, Leo felt a nagging unease in the back of his mind.

"Aisha, I appreciate our friendship, but I need to be honest. I'm committed to Bhargi, and I want to respect that," Leo said, his heart pounding.

Aisha nodded, but her eyes reflected a mix of emotions. "I understand, Leo. I just wish things were different. We have such a strong connection, and I can't help but feel like there's potential for something more."

Leo felt torn. He valued Aisha's friendship, but he also recognized the danger of crossing boundaries he had worked so hard to establish. "I care about you, but I can't jeopardize what I have with Bhargi," he replied firmly.

After dinner, Leo left feeling conflicted. Aisha's words echoed in his mind, and he struggled to reconcile his feelings. The tension between loyalty and attraction created a storm within him, and he found himself questioning the strength of his commitment to Bhargi.

Days turned into weeks, and the emotional turmoil continued to build. Leo immersed himself in work, pouring his energy into research, but the distraction only masked his internal struggle. He felt guilty for the thoughts that crept in, questioning whether he could truly maintain a long-distance relationship while navigating the complexities of life in London.

As Leo and Bhargi continued their video calls, he sensed her vulnerability in their conversations. She opened up about her own struggles, the challenges of being apart, and the longing she felt for him. Her words resonated deeply, but they also magnified Leo's guilt. He knew he had to be honest with her about the challenges he faced.

One evening, during one of their calls, Leo took a deep breath. "Bhargi, I need to talk to you about something," he began, his heart racing. "I've been struggling with the distance, and it's made me question a lot of things."

Bhargi's expression shifted, concern etched on her face. "What do you mean?"

"I want to be honest. Aisha and I have grown close, and I've been grappling with feelings that I didn't anticipate. I want you to know that you're my priority, but I feel torn," he admitted, his voice trembling.

The silence that followed felt heavy. Bhargi's eyes glistened with unshed tears. "Leo, I appreciate your honesty. But it hurts to hear that you're struggling. I thought we were committed to each other."

"We are, Bhargi. I care about you deeply, but I can't ignore the reality of what I'm feeling," Leo replied, his heart aching. "I don't want to hurt you, but I also don't want to lie."

Bhargi nodded, her expression a mixture of hurt and understanding. "I need some time to process this. It's hard to hear that you're feeling this way. I love you, Leo, and I thought we were building a future together."

As they ended the call, Leo felt a sense of relief and anguish. He had been honest, but the weight of uncertainty hung heavy in the air. He knew he had to navigate this crossroads carefully, for the love they had built deserved respect.

Over the next few days, Leo found himself reflecting on his feelings and the choices he had made. He realized that he had to take responsibility for his emotions. Aisha was a significant presence in his life, but he couldn't allow those feelings to cloud his commitment to Bhargi.

Determined to clarify his priorities, Leo reached out to Aisha for a frank conversation. They met at a park, and Leo felt the weight of his decision pressing down on him. "Aisha, we need to talk about our friendship," he began, his voice steady. "I value you, but I can't continue to navigate these feelings. I'm committed to Bhargi, and I want to respect that."

Aisha's expression shifted, a hint of disappointment flickering in her eyes. "I get it, Leo. I just wish things were different," she replied softly. "I really like you."

Leo felt the pang of regret but knew he had to stay true to his commitment. "I appreciate your understanding, Aisha. You deserve someone who can give you their full attention." They parted ways with a sense of resolution, and Leo felt lighter, knowing he had made the right choice.

As he returned to work, Leo focused on nurturing his relationship with Bhargi. They resumed their calls, discussing their dreams, their future, and the love that still bound them together. The distance remained a challenge, but he was determined to make it work, to prove that their love was worth the effort.

8

THE SHINING SUN -THE PROPOSAL

After a year of longing and searching, fate finally brought Leo and Sharmi together again. It was a day Leo would never forget. They met under the stars, just as they had dreamed. As they embraced, the walls Leo had built around his heart crumbled. He cried for the first time in years, and Sharmi held him as though she had been waiting for this moment all along.

One year after their fateful encounter on the plane, Leo finally heard from Sharmi.

It was a simple message—"Let's meet"—but those two words sent Leo's heart racing. After months of silence, of wondering if he would ever see her again, she was back. They arranged to meet at a small café near her apartment, and as Leo walked through the streets of London, his mind raced with anticipation.

When he saw her sitting at the table, waiting for him, it was as if no time had passed at all. Sharmi looked just as beautiful as he remembered, her smile soft and warm. And as they sat across from each other, talking and laughing like old friends, Leo realized something that had been buried deep inside him for years.

He still loved her.

Their reunion was bittersweet. Sharmi had been through her own struggles in the past year, but like Leo, she had never forgotten him. They talked for hours, catching up on everything that had happened since their last meeting. And by the end of the night, it was clear to both of them—they weren't just old lovers reconnecting. They were something more.

That night, Leo felt something he hadn't felt in years: peace.

Their love was undeniable, but their families didn't approve. Leo knew that being with Sharmi would mean defying expectations, breaking traditions, and leaving behind the life he had once imagined for himself. But he didn't care. He had found his heart again, and nothing else mattered.

Leo's life had been a chaotic whirlwind of flings, career ambitions, and restless nights spent searching for meaning. Despite achieving considerable success in his career as a neuroscientist, he often found himself grappling with a sense of emptiness. The relationships he had experienced over the past few years—casual and devoid of depth—had left him emotionally drained and numb.

His heart raced as he read her message. The stars had finally aligned.

When they met again, it was as if no time had passed. The connection between them was just as strong as it had been on the plane. But this time, there were no uncertainties. Leo knew that Sharmi was the one he had been waiting for, the one who could fill the void in his heart.

"I've missed you," Leo admitted as they sat together in a quiet café, the world outside bustling with activity.

"I've missed you too," Sharmi replied, her eyes filled with emotion.

From that moment on, Leo and Sharmi's relationship blossomed. They spent every possible moment together, rekindling the love they had once shared as children. For the first time in years, Leo felt truly at peace. Sharmi had brought him back to life, reminding him of what it meant to love deeply and wholeheartedly.

But their journey wasn't without challenges. Their families were opposed to their relationship, and they faced criticism from all sides. Yet, Leo was determined to fight for the love he had rediscovered. Together, they decided to leave behind the noise and start anew. They moved to New York, away from the pressures of family and society, to build a life of their own.

In New York, their love flourished. They built a home, started a family, and welcomed their daughter, Harshita, into the world. Leo had finally found the peace and happiness he had been searching for all his life. Sharmi was his anchor, his guiding star, and together, they created a life filled with love, joy, and purpose.

Leo's journey had come full circle—from a heartbroken young man searching for meaning in fleeting flings to a devoted husband and father who had found the love of his life. Sharmi had healed his heart, and together, they had built a future that was brighter than anything he could have imagined.

Leo's story of rediscovering love with Sharmi was the turning point that led him to embrace true connection and fulfillment, putting an end to his restless search. Their journey wasn't easy, but it was worth every moment of struggle, and together, they created a life built on love, trust, and the deep bond they had always shared.

The moment Leo locked eyes with Sharmi, everything changed. She was the love he had been missing, the innocence and warmth he had longed for but had buried under layers of pain and lust. Memories of his childhood flooded back, and in her embrace, the anger and chaos within him began to dissolve. For the first time in years, Leo felt his heart beat again.

But their love story wasn't meant to be easy. London was a vast city, and despite the deep connection between them, they struggled to find each other again. For a year, Leo lived his life in London, returning to his old ways of seeking pleasure and distraction. Sabar fueled his hunger for success, but Sharmi's absence left an emptiness within him.

One fateful day, everything shifted. Leo and Sharmi reunited after a year of being apart. Tears streamed down their faces as they embraced, and in that moment, Leo knew he had finally found the peace he had been searching for. The wolf within him quieted, and the love that had once eluded him returned with a force that left him breathless.

They moved in together, ready to build a future despite the resistance from their families. When the pressure became too much, Leo made a decision that would define the rest of his life. He and Sharmi would move to New York, away from the expectations and judgments, to start their new chapter.

9

HOWAY NEW YORK- TRIALS AND TRIUMPHS

In New York, Leo and Sharmi built a life together, and their love blossomed. They welcomed a daughter into the world, naming her Harshita, a symbol of the beauty that came from their hard-fought love. Leo's journey from heartbreak to redemption was complete, and as he held his family close, he realized that true success was not in the number of flings or accolades, but in the love that had survived despite it all.

Together, they lived happily ever after, their story a testament to the resilience of the human heart.

Leo and Sharmi's decision to move to New York had been an easy one in theory, but in practice, it was anything but simple.

They both knew they were running away from the disapproving glares of their families, from the societal expectations that weighed on them like a heavy cloud. It wasn't that they didn't love their families or respect the culture they had come from. They simply understood that if they were going to have any chance at happiness together, they had to carve out a space that was truly theirs.

New York was the city of new beginnings. For Leo, it was the place where he could finally focus on his growing career as a neuroscientist without the distractions that had plagued his life in India and London. Sharmi, with her calm and centered presence, quickly found work as a psychologist specializing in trauma counseling. Both of them were thriving professionally, and the city itself—with its towering skyscrapers, buzzing energy, and endless opportunities—felt like the ideal backdrop to the life they were trying to build.

In New York, Leo and Sharmi built a life that was all their own. They found peace in the chaos of the city, and their love only grew stronger.

Leo and Sharmi moved in together shortly after their reunion, and for the first time since his breakup, Leo felt like he had found his place in the world. Their relationship wasn't perfect—far from it. Both of them had scars from their pasts, and the road ahead wasn't easy. Their families were against their relationship, and the pressures of their careers weighed heavily on them.

But they had each other.

Eventually, Leo and Sharmi made the difficult decision to move to New York, away from the disapproving eyes of their families. It was a fresh start, a chance to build a life together on their terms. And when their daughter, Harshita, was born, it was the culmination of everything they had fought for.

Leo looked at his life, at his daughter's bright eyes and Sharmi's loving smile, and he realized that the wolf inside him had finally found peace. He had spent years chasing success, lust, and power, but in the end, it was love that had saved him.

Leo had built a life where no one could reject him. But in the process, he had discovered something far more important—he had built a life where he could finally accept himself.

And in that life, he had found happiness.

For Leo, Harshita was the culmination of his journey. She represented everything he had fought for, everything he had lost and found again. He had finally learned that success wasn't about the number of flings, the accolades, or even the achievements. It was about the people who loved him despite his flaws, the ones who stayed even when the wolf inside him had threatened to consume everything.

Together, Leo, Sharmi, and Harshita lived happily ever after. Their story was a testament to the power of love, resilience, and the human heart's ability to heal—even after it has been shattered.

But there were challenges, as there always are. As they settled into their new life, the early excitement of their move began to fade, and reality crept in. Leo and Sharmi were two strong personalities with their own ambitions, their own dreams, and their own ways of dealing with the world. At first, their differences were exciting. Sharmi's steady calm balanced out Leo's fiery passion, and they leaned on each other for support.

But as the months passed, they began to face the same struggles every couple does. Long work hours meant they didn't always have time for one another. Leo's job as a neuroscientist involved late nights in the lab, attending international conferences, and pushing himself to new heights in his research. Sharmi, meanwhile, was emotionally drained from helping her patients navigate their own traumas and found herself needing space to decompress at the end of the day.

Though their love for each other never wavered, cracks began to appear. There were small arguments—about things as mundane as household chores or how little time they had to spend together. But there were deeper issues too. Leo's fear of failure, of not living up to the lofty goals he had set for himself, began to weigh on him. He was constantly striving to be the best in his field, to achieve more than anyone had ever expected of him. This ambition, the same one that had once driven him to great heights, now began to consume him.

One night, after a particularly grueling week at work, Leo came home to find Sharmi sitting on the couch, her arms crossed and a look of concern on her face. She didn't say anything at first, but Leo could tell that something was wrong.

"Leo," she said softly, her voice tinged with a sadness he hadn't heard before. "We need to talk."

He dropped his bag by the door and sat down next to her, his heart heavy. He knew this conversation had been a long time coming.

"I feel like we're drifting apart," Sharmi said, her eyes searching his for understanding. "We've both been so focused on our careers, on achieving success, that we've stopped making time for each other. I miss us."

Leo sighed, running a hand through his hair. "I know. I've been feeling it too. But it's not like we're doing anything wrong, right? We're both just... busy."

Sharmi shook her head. "It's not just about being busy, Leo. It's about what we prioritize. We came here to build a life together, but lately, it feels like we're living two separate lives."

Her words stung, not because they were harsh, but because they were true. Leo had thrown himself into his work, using it as a way to avoid confronting the growing distance between them. He had always been a lone wolf, someone who thrived on the thrill of personal achievement, but he had forgotten that relationships required effort, just as much as any career did.

"I don't want to lose us," Sharmi continued, her voice breaking slightly. "But I also don't want to feel like I'm second place in your life."

Leo felt a lump rise in his throat. He had been so focused on becoming the best neuroscientist, on proving something to the world—and maybe to himself—that he had lost sight of what truly mattered. Sharmi wasn't asking him to give up his dreams or ambitions, but she needed to know that their relationship was just as important to him as his career.

"I don't want to lose us either," Leo said, his voice thick with emotion. "I've been so caught up in trying to succeed that I didn't realize how much I've been neglecting you... neglecting us."

Sharmi reached out and took his hand. "We don't have to have it all figured out, Leo. But we need to make time for each other, even when it's hard."

Leo nodded. "You're right. I've been so focused on the future that I've forgotten to be present with you."

That night, they made a promise to each other—a promise to prioritize their relationship, no matter how busy life became. They agreed to set aside time each week to reconnect, whether that meant going out on a date, taking a walk in Central Park, or simply sitting down for dinner together without any distractions. They both knew it wouldn't be easy, but they were committed to making it work.

As they worked through their issues, something shifted in their relationship. The cracks that had started to form began to heal, and they rediscovered the joy they had once found in each other's company. Sharmi's steady presence grounded Leo, helping him find balance in his life, while Leo's passion reignited the spark between them. They began to support each other not just as lovers, but as partners in the truest sense of the word.

Months passed, and Leo's career continued to flourish. He became known for his groundbreaking research in neuroscience, gaining recognition in academic circles around the world. But unlike before, Leo no longer measured his success solely by his professional achievements. He had learned that true success came from balance—balancing ambition with love, career with relationships, and personal growth with partnership.

As they approached their second year in New York, Sharmi surprised Leo with news that would change their lives forever. She was pregnant.

Leo was overjoyed, but along with the excitement came a new set of fears. Would he be a good father? Could he handle the responsibilities of parenthood while still pursuing his career? The doubts crept in, but Sharmi, as always, was there to reassure him.

"We'll figure it out, Leo," she said, her hand resting gently on her growing belly. "We've always figured things out together."

The months that followed were a whirlwind of preparation. They turned one of the rooms in their apartment into a nursery, filled with soft blankets, tiny clothes, and books that they hoped to one day read to their child. Leo spent hours researching parenting, determined to be the best father he could be. But no matter how much they prepared, nothing could have truly readied them for the day their daughter,

A year later, they welcomed a daughter into the world—a beautiful girl named Harshita. She was the perfect blend of both of them, a symbol of the love that had overcome all odds.

Harshita, was born.

Leo remembered the moment he held her for the first time. She was so small, so delicate, yet filled with so much life. In that instant, everything changed. All of his fears, his doubts, and his insecurities melted away. Holding Harshita in his arms, Leo felt a profound sense of purpose unlike anything he had ever experienced before.

Looking at Sharmi, exhausted but smiling beside him, Leo realized that this—his family—was what he had been searching for all along. Not the fleeting thrills of casual flings, not the endless pursuit of career success, but the deep, lasting love that came from building something real, something that mattered.

As they brought Harshita home and settled into their new roles as parents, Leo found himself growing in ways he hadn't anticipated. Parenthood was challenging, yes, but it was also filled with moments of pure joy and wonder. Every time Harshita smiled, every time she reached out for him, Leo felt his heart swell with love.

Together, he and Sharmi navigated the highs and lows of parenthood, learning as they went, leaning on each other for support. And through it all, their love grew stronger, more resilient, and more enduring than ever before.

Leo had finally found his peace. Not in the frantic pursuit of success, not in the fleeting thrill of desire, but in the quiet, steady love of his family. And for the first time in his life, he felt truly complete.

10

THE EVOLUTION OF LOVE

The birth of Harshita marked the beginning of a new era for Leo and Sharmi, one that was filled with fresh challenges, sleepless nights, and endless wonder. Parenthood changed them both in ways they hadn't anticipated. For Leo, it was as if the world had suddenly shifted its axis—everything that had once seemed important, like his career and personal ambition, now paled in comparison to the tiny, fragile life he and Sharmi had brought into the world.

In those early weeks, Leo often found himself gazing at Harshita as she slept, mesmerized by the quiet rise and fall of her chest. There was something so pure and innocent about her, something that made him feel both vulnerable and invincible at the same time. Holding her in his arms, he realized that his days of chasing after fleeting moments of satisfaction were over. This—his family, his daughter, his love for Sharmi—was the foundation of his life now.

Of course, as any new parent will attest, the transition wasn't always smooth. The first few months were a blur of diapers, midnight feedings, and exhaustion that seemed to seep into every corner of their lives. Leo and Sharmi often found themselves feeling overwhelmed, unsure if they were doing everything right. Harshita's cries in the middle of the night tested their patience, their resilience, and, at times, their relationship.

But amidst the chaos, there were moments of profound beauty. Like when Harshita smiled for the first time—a tiny, toothless grin that made every sleepless night worth it. Or when she wrapped her little fingers around Leo's thumb, holding on with surprising strength, as if to say, *I'm here, and I need you.* Those moments were magic, and they filled Leo with a sense of purpose he had never known before.

In the months following Harshita's birth, Leo began to reassess his priorities. For years, he had been consumed by his ambition, driven by a need to prove something to the world. He had thrown himself into his work, pouring all of his energy into becoming the best neuroscientist he could be. But now, with a family to care for, he realized that his career—while still important—was no longer the only thing that defined him.

Sharmi, too, underwent her own transformation. Motherhood suited her in a way that Leo hadn't expected. She had always been calm and composed, but now there was a new softness in her, a deep well of patience and love that seemed to radiate from her whenever she held Harshita. She had always been Leo's anchor, the one who kept him grounded, but now, watching her with their daughter, Leo saw her in a new light. She was strong, capable, and fiercely protective, but also gentle and nurturing.

They found themselves growing together in ways they hadn't before. Parenthood forced them to rely on each other in new ways, to communicate more openly, and to be more patient with one another. There were moments when the stress of balancing work and family life took its toll, when tempers flared and misunderstandings arose. But each time, they came back to the same realization: they were in this together, and their love was strong enough to weather any storm.

Leo's work as a neuroscientist continued to flourish, though he made a conscious decision to scale back his hours in the lab. He wanted to be present for Harshita's milestones—to witness her first steps, hear her first words, and be there for her as she grew. It wasn't an easy decision, especially for someone as driven as Leo, but it was the right one. For the first time in his life, he understood that success wasn't just about accolades or recognition. True success, he realized, was about finding balance—between work and family, ambition and love.

Sharmi was his partner in every sense of the word. They took turns caring for Harshita, splitting the responsibilities of parenthood as equally as they could. On weekends, they would take her to the park, where they watched in awe as she explored the world around her with wide-eyed curiosity. She loved the swings, the way they made her feel weightless, and every time Leo pushed her higher, her laughter echoed through the park, filling him with a joy he hadn't known he was capable of feeling.

As the months turned into years, Leo and Sharmi settled into their roles as parents, but they never forgot about each other. They made time for date nights, sneaking away for quiet dinners at their favorite restaurants or spending lazy Sunday mornings in bed, talking about everything and nothing. They laughed together, cried together, and supported each other through the highs and lows of life. Their love, once filled with the fiery intensity of youth, had evolved into something deeper, more enduring. It was a love built on trust, respect, and the shared experience of raising a family.

But life wasn't without its challenges. As Harshita grew older, she developed a fiery personality much like her father's. She was independent, headstrong, and unafraid to assert herself, even as a toddler. There were days when her temper tantrums tested Leo and Sharmi's patience to the limit, but they handled it together, learning as they went. They weren't perfect parents, and they didn't have all the answers, but they loved Harshita fiercely, and that, they knew, was enough.

The years flew by in a blur, and before they knew it, Harshita was starting school. Leo and Sharmi watched with pride as their little girl marched confidently into her classroom, her backpack almost as big as she was. It was a bittersweet moment for both of them—exciting to see their daughter growing up, but also a reminder of how quickly time was passing.

As Harshita settled into her new routine, Leo and Sharmi found themselves with more time to focus on each other again. They rediscovered the joys of simply being together, of having uninterrupted conversations and stolen moments of intimacy. They traveled when they could, exploring new cities and countries, always returning home with a renewed sense of connection. Their love, which had weathered the storms of early parenthood, was now stronger than ever.

But life, as it always does, had more tests in store for them.

One winter, when Harshita was around seven years old, Sharmi's mother fell ill. The news hit them hard, especially Sharmi, who had always been close to her family despite the distance. They made the difficult decision to temporarily relocate to India to be with her during her final months. It was a challenging time for their family—managing the emotional strain of illness while trying to provide stability for Harshita, who was old enough to understand that something was wrong, but too young to fully grasp the gravity of the situation.

Leo, ever the protector, did his best to support Sharmi through her grief. He took on more responsibilities at home, allowing Sharmi the time and space she needed to care for her mother and process her emotions. It wasn't easy, but they navigated the situation with the same strength and resilience that had carried them through so many other challenges.

After her mother's passing, Sharmi was understandably devastated, but Leo stood by her, offering quiet support and love in the ways he knew best. They leaned on each other, finding solace in the knowledge that they were not alone

11

LIFE AS PREDICTED A PERFECT ENDING

The years that followed Sharmi's mother's passing were a period of quiet healing. Life, in its relentless march forward, had taught Leo and Sharmi many things, but perhaps the most important lesson was how to endure—how to embrace the difficult moments without letting them break the bond they had forged over time. With each challenge they had faced, they had grown closer, not just as partners, but as a family.

Leo watched Harshita grow with an indescribable sense of pride. She was becoming everything he had hoped she would be: intelligent, compassionate, and fiercely independent. The fire that he had once carried in his own spirit, the insatiable hunger for life, had passed on to his daughter. She excelled in school, but more than that, she had a deep curiosity about the world, much like Leo himself when he was younger. Harshita was full of questions, always wanting to understand how things worked—from the simplest curiosities of childhood to the complexities of human nature. And every time she asked a question, Leo felt a swell of joy in sharing his knowledge with her.

Sharmi, ever the calm center of their family, had returned to her work as a psychologist. But something had shifted in her, a quiet peace that came from having faced her mother's death with grace. She had embraced the idea of living in the present—of cherishing the small moments rather than being consumed by what might come next. Leo often found her lost in thought while they sat together in the evenings, watching the sunset from the balcony of their apartment. She would smile at him, and in that smile, Leo saw all the love, all the history, all the life they had built together.

New York, once a city that had seemed so vast and full of unknowns, had become their home. It was where they had grown as individuals and as a couple, where they had raised their daughter, and where they had built a life rich with memories. Leo's career had reached new heights—he was now considered one of the foremost neuroscientists in the world, regularly publishing groundbreaking research and speaking at international conferences. But even as his professional accolades piled up, he no longer felt the relentless need to prove himself. His career was a part of him, but it no longer defined him.

One evening, many years after they had first moved to New York, Leo found himself standing in the kitchen, preparing dinner while Sharmi and Harshita talked in the living room. Harshita, now a teenager, was animatedly telling her mother about a project she was working on for school—something about neurobiology, a subject Leo had introduced her to years ago. Hearing the enthusiasm in her voice, Leo smiled to himself. His daughter was following in his footsteps, but not because he had pushed her. She had discovered her own love for science, and he couldn't be prouder.

As he chopped vegetables, Leo's mind wandered back to the journey that had led him here. He thought about the younger version of himself, the one who had been lost in a whirlwind of heartbreak, anger, and ambition. The boy who had turned to flings and fleeting passions to fill the void left by his first heartbreak. That boy had been searching—desperately seeking something to make him feel whole.

Leo realized now that he had been chasing the wrong things. The validation he had sought through women, through his career, had never been the answer. The real answer, the real peace he had found, had always been in the people he loved—Sharmi and Harshita.

He thought of Sharmi, the woman who had seen him through his darkest times, who had stood by him even when he didn't deserve it. She had been his anchor, his guide, and his partner in every sense of the word. Together, they had faced life's storms, but they had always come out stronger on the other side. Their love, once intense and passionate, had deepened into something far more profound—something built on trust, understanding, and the shared experience of building a life together.

Leo glanced into the living room, where Sharmi was laughing at something Harshita had said. The sound of her laughter filled the room, warm and full of life. In that moment, Leo knew—he had found everything he had ever wanted. He didn't need to chase anything anymore. He had already won the greatest prize of all.

That night, after dinner, Leo and Sharmi sat together on the balcony, watching the stars twinkle in the clear night sky. Harshita had gone to bed, her laughter still echoing in their minds.

"Do you remember when we first moved here?" Sharmi asked, her voice soft in the quiet night.

Leo nodded. "Feels like a lifetime ago."

Sharmi smiled, resting her head on his shoulder. "We've come a long way, haven't we?"

"We have," Leo agreed, wrapping his arm around her. He took a deep breath, feeling the weight of all those years settle into a peaceful contentment. "I wouldn't trade any of it."

Sharmi turned to look at him, her eyes filled with the same love and warmth he had seen from the first moment they reconnected in London. "Neither would I."

They sat in comfortable silence for a while, the city's hum a distant backdrop to their thoughts. For the first time in years, Leo felt completely at peace. He wasn't chasing anything anymore. He wasn't running from his past, nor was he trying to prove himself to anyone. He had everything he needed—right here, beside him.

As the cool breeze brushed past them, Sharmi whispered, "I love you, Leo."

He turned to her, smiling softly. "I love you too."

In that simple exchange, Leo felt the culmination of all their years together, all the trials they had faced, all the joy they had shared. It wasn't a grand declaration or a dramatic moment, but it was perfect in its simplicity. Their love had been tested and refined over time, and now it stood unshakable, a beacon of light in the ever-changing world around them.

The years ahead would undoubtedly bring new challenges, new adventures, and new moments of joy. But Leo knew, with absolute certainty, that whatever came next, they would face it together. Because, in the end, that was what mattered most—love, family, and the life they had built together.

And as they sat there under the stars, Leo realized that this was his perfect ending. Not in some far-off future or a distant dream, but right here, in this moment, with the woman he loved and the family they had created. His search was over. He had found his home.

And he was finally, truly, at peace.

The perfect ending wasn't about a single triumph, but the quiet, enduring love that carried them through everything. This was the life Leo had always wanted, the one he had never known he needed until he found it in Sharmi and Harshita. It was more than enough. It was everything.

www.ingramcontent.com/pod-product-compliance
Lightning Source LLC
LaVergne TN
LVHW061618070526
838199LV00078B/7337